Zonderkidz

Nervous Norman Hot on the Trail
Copyright © 2009 by Bill Meyers
Illustrations © 2009 by Andy J. Smith

Requests for information should be addressed to:
Zonderkidz, Grand Rapids, Michigan 49530

Library of Congress Cataloging-in-Publication Data

Myers, Bill, 1953-
 Nervous Norman hot on the trail / by Bill Myers ; [illustrations by Andy J. Smith].
    p. cm. -- (Bug parables)
 ISBN 978-0-310-71217-6 (printed hardcover) [1. A retelling of the parable of the lost sheep, in which a shepherd of ladybugs discovers how much God loves him. 2. Stories in rhyme. 3. Ladybugs--Fiction. 4. Lost children--Fiction. 5. Lost sheep (Parable)--Fiction. 6. Parables--Fiction. 7. Christian life--Fiction.] I. Smith, Andy J., 1975- ill. II. Title.
 PZ8.3.M99534Ne 2009
 [E]--dc22
                                                2008016961

All Scripture quotations unless otherwise noted are taken from the Holy Bible: New International Version®. NIV®. Copyright © 1973, 1978, 1984 by International Bible Society. Used by permission of Zondervan. All rights reserved.

All rights reserved. No part of this publication may be reproduced, stored in a retrieval system, or transmitted in any form or by any means—electronic, mechanical, photocopy, recording, or any other—except for brief quotations in printed reviews, without the prior permission of the publisher.

Published in association with the literary agency of Alive Communications, Inc., 7680 Goddard Street #200, Colorado Springs, CO 80920, www.alivecommunications.com.

Any Internet addresses (websites, blogs, etc.) and telephone numbers printed in this book are offered as a resource. They are not intended in any way to be or imply an endorsement by Zondervan, nor does Zondervan vouch for the content of these sites and numbers for the life of this book.

Zonderkidz is a trademark of Zondervan.

Editor: Betsy Flikkema
Art direction & design: Sarah Molegraaf

Printed in China

09 10 11 12 • 6 5 4 3 2 1

NERVOUS NORMAN HOT ON THE TRAIL

The Parable of the Lost Sheep

written by **BILL MYERS**

illustrated by **ANDY J. SMITH**

THE BUG PARABLES

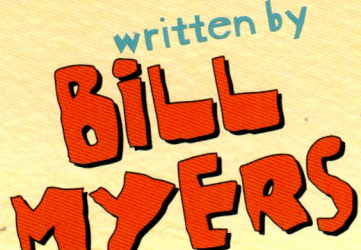
ZONDERkidz

ZONDERVAN.com/
AUTHORTRACKER
follow your favorite authors

He heads off and hires a slick private eye.

You're sure you can find her?

I'm the best money buys.

Their first stop is the schoolyard—
with swings and dodgeball.